ODD TO THE RESCUE!

James Roose-Evans

Odd is lonely as Elsewhere has gone to spend time with a travelling circus. He decides to spend his summer holidays with Farmer Thomas in Wales, but on arrival he discovers that Bear Mountain has been taken over by a wicked enemy, Malevil, who has imprisoned his friend, the Great Bear. The prison can be reached by secret underground passages which only the brave Odd is small enough to squeeze through. But will he be able to rescue the Great Bear in time?

JAMES ROOSE-EVANS

ODD TO THE RESCUE!

AN ODD & ELSEWHERE STORY WITH PICTURES BY BRIAN ROBB

A Magnet Book

Also by James Roose-Evans in Magnet Books:

THE ADVENTURES OF ODD AND ELSEWHERE
THE SECRET OF THE SEVEN BRIGHT SHINERS
ODD AND THE GREAT BEAR
ELSEWHERE AND THE CLOWNS

Other Books about Odd and Elsewhere are:

THE SECRET OF TIPPITY-WITCHET
THE LOST TREASURE OF WALES

Published by André Deutsch

First published in Great Britain 1975
by André Deutsch Ltd, under the title
The Return of the Great Bear
Magnet paperback edition published 1983
by Methuen Children's Books Ltd,
11 New Fetter Lane, London EC4P 4EE
Copyright © 1975 James Roose-Evans
Illustrations © 1975 Brian Robb
All rights reserved
Printed in Great Britain by
Richard Clay (The Chaucer Press) Ltd,
Bungay, Suffolk

ISBN 0 416 45170 5

THIS, THE FIFTH OF THE SEVEN BOOKS
OF ODD AND ELSEWHERE,
IS SPECIALLY FOR

KATHERINE

WHO
WROTE ME MY FIRST FAN LETTER
AND SENT ME A PENCIL
WITH WHICH TO
WRITE MORE STORIES
ABOUT ODD AND ELSEWHERE

Fenton House in Hampstead, London,
belongs to the National Trust, and is
open to the public. The National Trust,
which was founded in 1894, helps to
save and preserve the nation's historic
houses, castles, gardens and thousands
of acres of land that might otherwise be
lost or destroyed.

'Indeed to goodness, Odd!' exclaimed Collander Moll, looking up from her darning (she was mending his second best pair of blue jeans). 'It's nearly two o'clock. I thought you told Elsewhere you were going up the hill to see the circus this afternoon?'

Odd stared up at the clock on the mantelpiece; he had never been very good at telling the time. 'Oh, my goodness, oh, my oddness!' he replied.

He trotted up the hill from Fenton House, where he and Elsewhere lived with Collander Moll who was the housekeeper, and Hallelujah Jones who was the gardener and also Moll's father.

As Odd crossed the road by Whitestone Pond at the top of Heath Street he saw a line of charabancs. They were crowded with children, coming from Kilburn and Finchley, Islington and Highbury, Chalk Farm and Paddington, especially to see the circus. All the children waved at Odd as he trotted past. Ever since he and Elsewhere had captured the famous gang of thieves known as The Seven Bright Shiners, and had appeared on television and had their pictures in the newspapers,

7

they had been famous.

'Where's Elsewhere?' the children chorused, but Odd just waved and hurried on down the hill towards the Vale of Health where he could see the big top outlined against the sky and could hear the sound of loud cheerful music.

At the entrance to the tent was a giant model of a clown's head and shoulders. The face was stretched in a great grin. In the centre was a flight of red steps sticking out like a tongue. The audience climbed these steps and passed through the mouth of the clown in order to reach their seats inside the tent. On either side of the carnival head, forming a semicircle, were the arms and hands. Inside one giant hand was a stall selling cokes, fizzy drinks, and ice-creams. Inside the other was the box-office. It was here that Odd found Elsewhere, busily selling tickets for that afternoon's performance. Because he was to be the next King of the Clowns, Elsewhere had made up his mind to find out

all he could about the way a circus is run.

'You see,' he had explained to Odd, 'although I've worked in a circus all my life as a clown, I've never had to think about anything except my own act. But now, if I am to be a good king, it's very important that I should know how to do everything from selling tickets to putting up a big top or mending a tear in the roof!'

And that was why he had taken a job with one of the biggest circuses in England, travelling all round the country, from Land's End to John o' Groats. The two performances that day on Hampstead Heath were the first of the season after which Odd knew that he probably would not see his friend for several months.

When the last of the audience had gone into the tent, Odd slipped inside the box-office to talk with Elsewhere. He noticed how dirty his white gloves had become from handling all the coins.

'Aren't you on at the beginning?' he asked, swinging his legs as he sat on the thumb of the giant hand.

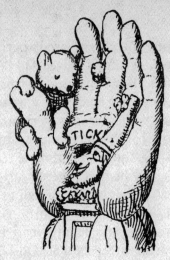

'No,' answered Elsewhere. 'I've got fifteen minutes before I have to stand in for Abu, the Elephant Boy.'

'Why, where is he?' asked Odd.

'He's in plaster!' answered Elsewhere. 'He fell off the big elephant when they were rehearsing this morning and he's cracked three of his ribs. So, as the Guv'nor says I haven't got a bone in my body, it was decided I should stand in for Abu until his bones are set.'

'Can I watch?' asked Odd excitedly, slipping down from the thumb.

'Yes, only you won't recognise me by the time I've finished making-up,' answered Elsewhere. 'And then, after that, it's the interval when I've got to sell ice-creams. You can help me with that if you like,' he added, looking across at Odd. 'My own act's in the second half, although I have to be prepared to go on for almost anyone if they're sick or have an accident. I'm the general stand-in.'

'Would you have to go on as the lion-tamer if he were sick?' asked Odd.

'Oh, I expect so!' answered Elsewhere cheerfully. 'I'd

just give the lions lots to eat before they went on so that they wouldn't want to eat me!'

He dropped the shutter over the box-office window. 'Then at the end of the show,' he continued, 'I have to help sweep up all the empty ice-cream cartons and sweet-papers before the next performance. Tonight we take down the big top and pack everything up ready for an early start in the morning. I'll be leaving first as I have to go ahead with the Guv'nor's son, checking that all the advance publicity is in order, and the site ready for when the main party arrives.'

He grinned. 'There's never a dull moment! You have to be prepared to turn your hand to almost anything.'

Odd gazed at his friend in wonder. Elsewhere seemed altogether a different person, quite content to do all these tasks cheerfully because he knew that only in this way could he become a knowledgeable and wise king.

'Where are you taking that?' asked Odd, seeing him pour all the money into a large canvas bag. He had never seen so much money. Elsewhere staggered beneath the weight.

'I'm going to put it in the safe in the Guv'nor's caravan. You can come with me if you like, and after that you can watch me make-up.'

By the time Elsewhere had blackened his face with grease-paint, put on white trousers, a white jacket with a high collar buttoning up to the neck, and a brilliantly coloured turban on top of his head, Odd could not recognise his friend. All he could see was Abu, the Elephant Boy. He stared at a bright twinkling jewel in the centre of the turban, as large as a hen's egg and as red as a ruby.

'Is that real?' he asked in a hushed voice.

Elsewhere laughed. 'It's what they used to call paste jewellery,' he answered. 'It's made of perspex nowadays, however. It's what they use for films and television. At a distance, under the lights, it looks exactly like the real thing. You wait till you see Suzie – that's the Guv'nor's wife – at the finale when she rides round on a white Arab horse. She's covered from head to foot in diamonds; tiara, necklace, armlets, anklets, and hundreds sewn into her costume – they twinkle under the lights and you'd think they were priceless diamonds. But they're all false!'

Odd listened in awe. It all seemed such a different world to him, not at all his kind of scene. Yet he realised that this was where Elsewhere belonged. All his life, until recently, had been spent in one circus or another, travelling about the world. Then, for a while, he had been forgotten. That was when Odd had first met him. Now he understood why Elsewhere had been so restless and he realised how much he must have missed all this excitement, the hustle and bustle, the feeling of here today and gone tomorrow. It's like gipsies, he thought; they're always on the move.

'Are you coming then, man?' called Elsewhere in a voice that sounded exactly like Abu, the Indian boy. Odd laughed. Then Elsewhere added in his own voice, 'You can stand in the wings and watch the elephants!'

Once upon a time Odd had always been on his own. Until Elsewhere had come along. Then they had always done everything together, except for the time when Odd had gone off on his own to Wales in search of the Great Bear. Now, left suddenly to himself again, he felt very restless. He wandered about the house and garden, not knowing what to do.

'Why don't you take a holiday?' suggested Collander Moll one morning at breakfast.

Odd was banging the top of his egg with a spoon to crack the shell.

'You might have some more adventures,' she added.

'Yes, that would be fun,' agreed Odd, peeling off the shell and revealing the shiny white of the egg inside. 'But where would I go?'

'Well, there's my auntie in Llandrindod Wells,' suggested Collander Moll. 'Or Mr Goodman and his friend Arbuthnot.'

'Or Farmer Thomas and his family,' suggested Hallelujah, looking up from lighting his pipe.

'In fact, come to think of it,' added Collander Moll,

'there's a lot of friends you have now just. There's lovely it is. Well, that's settled then!'

Odd looked up, startled. It was almost as though Collander Moll wanted to get rid of him.

'I might change my mind!' he announced, testing her out. 'I might just go as far as Euston Station and then come back.'

'Oh, I don't trouble!' replied Collander Moll cheerfully. 'Just do what you feel like. That's what a holiday is for, isn't it?'

Odd made a dab at his egg with the spoon. This was always the tricky bit. If you were not careful the spoon went in too quickly and the yolk spurted out all over the table.

'Who knows but you might meet up again with the Great Bear,' added Hallelujah, clearing his throat and spitting into the fire. The fire spat back at him.

'Oh, Dad, I do wish you wouldn't do that,' clucked Collander Moll. 'You'll only put the fire out!'

Odd dipped a finger of bread and butter into the runny yolk and lowered it carefully into his mouth.

'Yes,' continued Hallelujah, pretending not to hear Collander Moll, 'you might well meet up with your old friend, the Great Bear.'

Odd looked across the table at Hallelujah. 'It's funny you should say that,' he murmured, his mouth full of egg, 'because I've been thinking a lot about him lately. Sometimes, in the middle of the night, I lie awake and

wonder – shall I ever see him again?'

Hallelujah's eyes twinkled above his spectacles as he looked across at Odd. It was he who had first told Odd about the Great Bear who had been a friend of Merlin, the Welsh wizard. Merlin had entrusted the Great Bear with the secret of where the lost Treasure of Wales was hidden. The Great Bear, guarding his secret, had fallen asleep in his stone hut on the top of Bear Mountain.

Over the centuries many had tried to find the mountain and claim the treasure for themselves but none had succeeded until Odd came.

The sound of a wasp buzzing, awakened by the early spring sunshine, roused Odd from his thoughts. Outside, on a cherry tree, a robin sang. Through the open door wafted a smell of daffodils and damp grass. It was a good time to be going again on a journey and before Collander Moll started her spring-cleaning. Once that began, everything and everybody got turned topsy-turvy.

'You've got egg on your chin!' interrupted Collander Moll sharply. 'Now if you've finished I'll clear the table!' With that she gathered up the table-cloth by its four corners so that plates, knives and forks, marmalade, teapot, all clattered and fell together into a squashy broken mess in the bottom. At once Odd recognised the mad look in Collander Moll's eyes. When she spoke sharply and began to behave oddly it was a sure sign that her spring-cleaning fever had started. Hallelujah winked at Odd as though to say – yes, it is definitely time to take to the road – and then hurriedly pocketed his spare pipes and the supplies of dried coltsfoot which he smoked for tobacco, before they all got thrown into the dust-bin.

Odd emptied out his savings from his money-box which was made of polished wood, shaped like a house with a chimney at one end, and painted with doors and windows. Collander Moll stuffed his satchel full of food.

'Where will you go then, lad?' asked Hallelujah Jones.

'To Farmer Thomas's,' replied Odd.

Hallelujah nodded. 'Right then. We'll telephone and say you're coming so that they can expect you. Never take people unawares.'

'What about your scarf?' called Collander Moll. 'Will you be needing that?'

'Oh, yes, I nearly forgot. Very useful a scarf, for lassoing horses, climbing trees, and tying up gangsters!'

He grinned.

Collander Moll sighed, shaking her head. 'Something odd about him. He's not quite centre,' she muttered to herself. 'Must be spring-fever gone to his head!'

With that she turned back into the kitchen and swept everything off the mantelpiece into the wastepaper-basket. 'There's tidier that is now!' she laughed.

Odd caught a train from Euston Station, changing at Rugby, changing at Wolverhampton, and changing again at Shrewsbury. Here he got on to a small diesel train with only two carriages. This was the mid-Wales line that went all the way to Swansea.

The track wound its way in and out of small valleys, or along steep mountain sides, the houses below looking like wooden toys. At many of the stations there was no longer a station-master so that if anyone wanted to board the train at any of these stations he had to signal the driver to stop. Sometimes, on misty or foggy mornings, the train would rattle by without stopping. At least that is what local people always claimed.

Wa–wa–wa–WAH! went the warning hooter as the train rounded a bend. Odd sat in the front seat so that he could watch the controls through the glass panel. The driver and his mate chatted, drinking tea out of a chipped enamel canister. They winked at Odd.

Dring–dring–dring! rang the bell as they passed a man on the side of the track stoking a bonfire of orange flames and black smoke. In the fields, down in the valley, blue tractors and red tractors were harrowing ploughed fields.

Thump–thump–thump! rattled the train like a man coming downstairs in heavy hobnail boots.

Phumf–a–phumf! blew the hooter as it passed a lonely signal-box.

Ba–ba–ba–BAH! bleated the train as it went through a short tunnel. On the other side, as they came out, were seven workmen in orange jackets repairing the line. They stood aside as the train shouted, *Foot–a–foomp!*

Odd jumped up and down with excitement. He thought that one day he would like to be an engine

20

driver.

For a while he leaned out of the window, watching the back and front of the train curving like a snake. Suddenly, just ahead of him, he noticed something dark being raised at an angle. Was it a signal? The train gave a sigh, *Ch–sss–Ch–sss!* and began to slow down. They were approaching a tiny station. There was a line of washing stretched across the platform – shirts and dresses filled with wind. Hens pecked at weeds growing out of cracks in the flagstones. Now he could see that the signal was the upraised arm of a man, and then, as the train drew alongside the platform, he saw that it was Farmer Thomas come to meet him. When Odd had set off on his first journey to find the Great Bear, and had been pursued by villains, it was Farmer Thomas who had come to his aid and helped him to get to Bear Mountain.

'Hullo there!' he called now, pushing his hat to the back of his head, his blue eyes smiling. 'The missis and all the children were right pleased to hear you were coming. And besides,' he added with a grin, 'we could do with some extra help! It's always a busy time now – lambing time. At least we've had no snow this year. Most years it always seems to snow just when ewes are lambing.'

The Land-Rover drove fast along the narrow twisting lanes, the banks already flowering with cow parsley. Suddenly rain began to splash against the windscreen, dribbling down so swiftly that Farmer Thomas had to switch on the wipers.

'We could do with some rain,' he observed. 'It's been very dry of late.'

Odd, peering out, said, 'Haven't we gone past the turning to the farm? Isn't that Bear Mountain ahead of us?'

'Aye, and there's something funny going on up there. Some big mining company has got Government permission to sink shafts and open it up for iron-ore. There's been a lot of protest from folks round about as well as in the posh newspapers, but the company that's taken it over seems to be very powerful and some folks think they must be hand in glove with the Government. The managing director is a man named Malevil. No one knows much about him, or where he's sprung from, but he seems to be pretty ruthless. Anyway, they've already started blasting. What's also made them unpopular is that they won't employ local people. They've brought in their own staff, and a rum lot they be.'

He paused and Odd could see that he was not only tired but worried.

'I thought we'd have a look round and spy out the land now that you are here. I wouldn't mind betting it's the treasure they're really after. I don't believe there's iron-ore in any of these mountains else there'd have been mining here long before this. But what really worries me is – what can have happened to our friend, the Great Bear? How does he fit into all this?'

Odd looked up at Farmer Thomas. 'Haven't you heard from him at all?' he asked.

Farmer Thomas shook his head. 'Not since the morning he brought you back,' he replied.

The rain was driving fast now, like steel needles. The windscreen was a blur of wetness so that they had difficulty in seeing the edges of the road. It was like trying to drive through a waterfall. As they approached the foot of the mountain, large notices loomed up at them out of the mist. Each bore a warning:

KEEP OUT!
DANGER!
STRICTLY PRIVATE
HIGH EXPLOSIVES

Suddenly their way was blocked. A barricade of wooden frames and barbed-wire extended across the road. To one side was a wooden sentry-box and from this there emerged a uniformed guard. On his cap was the design of a single staring eye.

'This is private property!' he shouted. 'Can't you read? Can't you see you are trespassing?'

Even as the guard spoke, Farmer Thomas was reversing and turning the Land-Rover around.

'Get in the back and hide!' he hissed to Odd. 'Whatever happens, keep out of sight.'

The guard came running, notebook in hand. 'Who are you?' he screamed.

As soon as Odd was out of sight, Farmer Thomas braked and leaned out of the window to speak to the guard who was standing with the rain cascading down his face.

'Beth ydych chw'in dweud?' asked Farmer Thomas in Welsh, which means – What did you say?

'Can't you speak English?' bellowed the guard, his notebook now drenched. 'What is your name? Who are you? I'll have you arrested for trespassing!'

Farmer Thomas scratched his head, pretending to be stupid, and looking as though he did not understand English.

24

'Oh, never mind,' replied the guard, moving round to the back of the vehicle. 'I'll soon get your number.'

Immediately Farmer Thomas pressed hard on the accelerator and, with a slither on the wet surface, the Land-Rover shot forward. The guard cursed as mud spattered all over him and his notebook fell in a puddle. By the time he had picked himself up, the Land-Rover had gone.

'Barbarians!' he shouted. 'Ruddy Welsh barbarians!'

Only when they had turned in to the lane that led to the farm, did Farmer Thomas slow down.

'You can come on out now, Odd!' he grinned. 'I doubt if he got our number, for one thing the number plate at the back is caked with mud. But I had a hunch you ought not to be seen. There's something very nasty going on up there, else why should they want to keep people out? And if it's to do with the treasure, as I think it is, then you've got to lie low until we find out what's best to do. If only we knew whether the Great Bear went back to the Mountain or not. Somehow we've got to find out where he is and get a message to him!'

The Great Bear had been very upset that he had forgotten where the treasure was hidden, even though Odd seemed not to mind.

'After all,' the Great Bear muttered to himself, 'what's the point of my keeping guard over it all these hundreds of years if when the time comes I've forgotten where it is!'

So he had gone back to his stone hut on the top of Bear Mountain and started to search through the hundreds of dusty old books he kept there, hoping to find a copy of Merlin's notes on where he had hidden the treasure. Of course, even if there were a copy, which he very much doubted, it would be in code, and as like as not he would have forgotten the key to it. However, he went on looking. But reading is tiring, especially when your eyesight is not very good. The Great Bear tried very hard to stay awake, however, because the last time he had fallen asleep it had been for centuries. But quite soon he was fast asleep in his armchair in front of a fire of peat turves.

Suddenly he was wide-awake. The fire had gone out

and the room felt cold and damp. Everywhere there were spiders' webs like miniature fishing nets. There was even one on the end of his nose. He found he could not see very well and wondered whether his eyesight was beginning to fail altogether. It would not be surprising he thought. After all, if one lives to be so old . . . The dust tickled his nose and he sneezed. The sudden movement knocked his spectacles sideways and then he realised why he had not been able to see. They were thick with dust. Wiping them clean with an end of his long scarf he murmured to himself, 'Dear me, dear me! I must have been asleep longer than I thought. I wonder what century I am in now?'

Thoughtfully he nibbled the other end of his scarf, peering round the room. What on earth was it that had woken him?

'Dear me, I can't even remember what it was that woke me!'

Then he heard it again and at once his heart began to pound. Now he remembered. It was the baying of hounds, a sound that had haunted bears for hundreds of years. For a moment he was so frightened that he could not move. It had been dogs that had nearly torn him to pieces all those years ago when he had been tied to a tree in a bear garden and the people had hurled stones at him. Then they had set the dogs on him. The people had been all round in a circle, separated by a fence, shouting and cheering and taking bets. One face he remembered most clearly, the thin cruel features of a man who had thrown pepper in his eyes to blind him so that he could not see to defend himself against the dogs. Snarling and slavering they had leaped on him, their teeth wrenching at his flesh, tearing it away.

Often, in his long sleep, the Great Bear had been
haunted by that thin cruel face, the face of his chief
tormentor many centuries ago.

If Merlin had not rescued him he would have been
dead. It was Merlin who had healed his wounds, except
for those in his feet – 'There my magic cannot help
thee,' he had said; 'thou must learn to live with some
pain.' Merlin had taken him to be his assistant and to

live, at the court of King Arthur.

The sound of the baying was louder now, rousing him
from his memories. He stretched his limbs and got up
experimentally, slowly testing his legs. They had gone
to sleep as well and were not yet as wide-awake as the
rest of him. But as he shuffled his way to the window
they began to hurt which meant that at last the blood
was circulating.

He pushed aside the many cobwebs that hung like folds of dark grey curtains at the one window, but the stretched pig's skin that served as a pane of glass was so thick with dirt that he could not see out. He spat on an end of his scarf and rubbed vigorously with it until he had cleared a small patch, the size of a peep-hole. Stooping, he placed an eye close up to it and found himself looking straight into another eye on the outside. For a moment the two eyes stared at each other, and then the one on the other side of the window vanished.

The next moment the door was kicked open; hounds surged into the room followed by men in uniforms, armed with guns. Each of the men wore a cap on the front of which was the image of a single staring eye. The Great Bear retreated to a corner while the men kicked and cursed at the dogs, hauling them off. Two of the guards seized the Great Bear, binding his arms tightly with ropes, while another crossed to the open door and called out to someone outside, 'He's here! We've got him!'

Outside the hut someone had thrown meat to the dogs to quieten them. Inside, the Great Bear, who in the struggle had lost his spectacles, closed his eyes and tried to shut out the image of those dogs with their long ears, slavering jaws, and bloodshot eyes.

He heard the door of the hut open and close. Someone had entered the room. Then a quiet voice spoke and its quietness was at once more terrifying than all the baying of the hounds. It was a voice totally without feeling, a voice so cold it made the Great Bear shiver.

'I hardly expected to find Ursus Major, the Great Bear, living in a pigsty,' purred the voice. 'Such filth, such a stench, is positively barbaric. But then, of course, you are a barbarian, are you not?'

At that moment the Great Bear recognised the voice. He had heard such voices before but this was the voice of the one who had tormented him most of all. It was the voice of his most dreaded enemy, and Merlin's also. It was the voice of Malevil himself.

The Great Bear opened his eyes and peered at the figure before him, standing with a magnificent hound at his side, held tightly on a short leather strap.

'And what would you do, Malevil,' he answered, 'without barbarians to torture?'

Stooping, Malevil picked up the Great Bear's spectacles and handed them back to him.

'Perhaps you are right,' he replied. 'Perhaps we need the barbarians to teach us manners.'

Putting on his spectacles (the glass in one frame had cracked), the Great Bear looked closely at his enemy.

Although dressed differently he had not changed in any other respect. But the unforgettable feature of that cruel face was the eyes. One he had lost in battle years ago and the closed lids, curving inwards, formed a thin red line in the hollowed socket, while the other protruded from its socket unnaturally. There seemed to be hardly any flesh on that face or body; it was all bone and a single, staring eye.

Malevil said something to the guards in a language which the Great Bear did not understand or recognise. At once he was released from his bonds and the guards left the hut. One of them returned with a battery lamp which was placed on the table, its light shining upwards, on to the cobwebbed rafters hung with canisters of dried fruit, nuts, and mushrooms; bunches of dried herbs; and ropes of onions. The two sat on either side of the table, their faces in shadow.

'And what now?' asked the Great Bear.

'Why, the Treasure, of course!' replied Malevil. 'You are to be held prisoner until you have shown us where it is hidden.'

'But I can no longer remember where it is hidden, that is just the point.'

'Then we shall have to see what we can do about improving your memory, shall we not?' replied Malevil. 'We have, over the centuries, perfected a variety of ways of getting people to talk. You'd be surprised how the most absent-minded of persons suddenly remembers!'

'And supposing I still do not speak?' answered the Great Bear. 'After all, once before, in the bear-garden, you did not succeed in destroying me.'

'Then our methods were crude and clumsy. Then, too – I freely admit it – we were barbarians. But now we have had time to perfect our methods and weapons. And besides my followers are now legion.'

The Great Bear snorted. He hated this kind of pompous talk.

'You think I boast?' snapped Malevil, nettled by the Great Bear's scorn. 'You would be advised to take me seriously.'

The Great Bear began to laugh. At first it was a heaving sound like someone with a bronchial cough. Then it grew, until, his spectacles slipping off his nose, the tears running down his hairy cheeks, the Great Bear was roaring with laughter.

Malevil rose, bewildered and angry.

The Great Bear, blowing his nose with one end of his scarf and wiping his eyes with the other, settled his spectacles again on his nose. 'Dear me, dear me!' he sighed. 'I'm afraid you are going to waste an awful lot of time because, you see, I really have forgotten where the Treasure is. That is the truth.'

'You lie!' snarled Malevil. 'This is your ursine cunning to try and throw me off the scent. But you will not succeed!'

He rose abruptly, his face disappearing into the darkness outside the lamp. Malevil's dog began to bark, straining at the leash. He called to the guards outside.

'Set Plan O.U.M. into operation at once!' he snarled.

The Great Bear looked at him over the top of his spectacles. 'O.U.M.?' he queried.

'*Operation Ursus Major*, of course!' replied Malevil coldly. 'We have had plenty of time to prepare for this day and we have devised a series of tortures especially for you. I trust you will find it worthy of anything your master, Merlin, could have conjured up.' With that he turned and left the hut.

Once again, as so many times in the past, the Great Bear was on his own.

By the time Odd and Farmer Thomas had reached the farm the rain had stopped. From inside the great barn they could hear the voices of children.

'It's Dad!' called out one.

'That means Odd will have arrived!' replied Mrs Thomas, and the next moment all the children appeared with their mother at the door of the barn to greet Odd.

Stephen, the youngest, seized him by the paw, dragging him inside. Hurdles, placed cross-wise, divided the space into pens for the young lambs whose mothers had died or had disowned them. Two were lying on a pile of straw, bleating, unable to get up.

'Rover was rough with them, and broke their legs,' explained Stephen in his husky, croaky voice. Stephen was six. He climbed on to the rungs of a hurdle, pulling Odd up beside him, and held out a feeding bottle full of milk towards a lamb that was unsteady on its legs.

'He's only two days old,' said Stephen, 'and Dad says he's mine!'

The lamb tugged at the rubber teat of the bottle, splashing milk in drops.

36

'He's called Greedy Guts!' laughed Stephen. 'I've got names for them all,' he explained. 'There's Jumbo and Dumbo and Sambo and . . .'

'And there's Daisy,' added his sister Jane, jumping up and down excitedly. 'And Lucy and Susy and Gracey and . . .'

'That's enough, Jane!' called her mother quickly. 'Have you finished feeding just? Because if so, will you go and put the supper on? I daresay Odd will be hungry after his long journey. All the way from London.'

The children looked across at Odd. London seemed a long way away. That was where the Queen and the Prime Minister lived. They had never been to London.

'Did you come in an aeroplane?' asked Allen.

'No, he came in a blunderbus!' shouted Andrew.

'Or a helicopter?' asked Jane.

'No, I came on a train!' laughed Odd. 'It went like this:

> Wa–wa–wa–*wah!*
> Dring–dring–dring!
> Thump–thump–thump!'

With that they all lined up behind Odd, holding on to each other's waists. They galloped out of the barn, round the yard, shouting, *Dring–dring–dring!*

Phumph–a–phumf! they went as they entered the back door.

Ba–ba–ba–BAA! they bleated through the scullery.

Foot–a–foomp! they shouted as they trotted along the passage. And then, as they entered the kitchen, they all slowed down with a big hissing, *Ch–sss! Ch–sss!*

During supper the children asked Odd so many questions that he had almost no time to eat. And although none of them had met Elsewhere they all felt they knew him and wanted to hear how he was getting on. Finally, Mrs Thomas entered with a big steaming pudding, like a sand-castle, which she set down in the centre of the table. Running down the sides and forming a puddle all round it was hot treacle.

'It's Treacle Pudding, especially in honour of Odd!' announced Mrs Thomas. 'Now you've all got to be

quiet while he eats it.'

'But it's not all for me?' gasped Odd, gazing at the steaming, golden pudding.

Mrs Thomas laughed. 'No, but you're to have first helping—'

'And second!' cried Jane.

'And third!' added Stephen.

They watched intently as Mrs Thomas slipped the

knife into the side of the crumbling, oozing mound, and cut a large slice for Odd. As soon as she had done this they all held up their plates, and banged their spoons, crying, 'Me next! Me next!'

Faced with a circle of waving plates, Mrs Thomas laughed as she dished out the pudding in treacly spoonfuls.

'Watch out there, Allen!' she cried. 'You'll have treacle all over your hair!'

Everybody had firsts and seconds, and Odd had a third helping. When they had finished they helped lick the big plate and then the smaller plates, until Mrs Thomas laughed and said, 'Now I shan't have any washing up to do!'

After supper they played hide-and-seek until it was time for them to go to bed. It was then that Farmer Thomas, his brother Dai and Odd sat quietly talking on the old bench outside the back door, under the light of a sickle moon that hung over Brockland Forest. Beyond, in the distance, they could see Bear Mountain.

Farmer Thomas told his brother what had happened earlier that afternoon and how he felt they must try and get a message to the Great Bear.

'Well, you can't do nothing now until the morning,' said Dai.

'That's true,' replied his brother, Albert. 'However, in the morning we might see if there's a way we can get past the guards, although somehow I don't think that's going to prove likely. And anyway we'd be no match for them.'

'But if the Great Bear is in trouble,' said Odd, 'we must do something. And if he's not on Bear Mountain then we ought to try and find out where he is and let

him know what's going on.'

Farmer Thomas sighed. 'That's just the trouble,' he said, 'We don't know where to look!'

'But we could start by seeing if he is on the mountain,' insisted Odd.

They sat in silence for a while. Then Farmer Thomas spoke again. 'Our Dad always says, when you've got a problem and you can't see your way round it, the best thing is to sleep on it. That way you often wake up in the morning with the answer!'

He rose. 'Time for your shut-eye, young man!' he said to Odd. 'You'll find your old bed made up in the attic.'

At that moment there was a clatter of footsteps on the flagstones and Mrs Thomas appeared with a flask of tea. 'I've made this up for you, Albert,' she said. 'And there's plenty of bread and cheese in the pantry if you want it later.'

Odd looked up at him questioningly.

'It's my turn to be up all night,' he explained. 'Dai did it last night. Like as not we'll have thirty lambs born tonight. About three in the morning I'll be glad of a hot cup of tea!'

He grinned, and taking a lantern, strode on down towards the big barn, followed in silence by Rover, the sheepdog.

'I don't know about you, young man,' yawned Dai, 'but I'm about ready to turn in.

Odd climbed up through the trapdoor in the floor to his room in the attic. For a while he sat up in bed, looking out at the mountains under the light of the moon. The furthest one, its peak swathed in mist, was Bear Mountain.

One by one the stars appeared in the sky. He could see the constellation of the Great Bear and, to one side, of the Little Bear.

'O Great Bear!' he murmured quietly, 'Wherever you are, help us to find you!'

And with that he fell asleep.

Just beyond the Great Bear's hut, where the rock levelled out, was a small lake. On the banks of this an enormous circular cage of aluminium frames had been erected, rather like an igloo with the top sliced off. In the centre of this a pine tree, its branches lopped away, had been driven like a stake deep into the rock. The Great Bear had been tied to this with ropes, his feet wedged painfully on two projecting stumps. All through the night, arc-lamps, driven by electric generators, had shone brilliantly down on the cage, attracting hundreds of moths like circling gnats, and dazzling the Great Bear whose eyes, like those of all bears, were not very strong.

Leading to the cage was a runway with a series of metal gates operated by pulleys. At the far end of this tunnel were the waiting hounds. Every six hours one of the gates would be raised, bringing the hounds gradually closer and closer to the Great Bear. He calculated that he had exactly thirty-six hours before the final gate was raised and he would be torn to pieces by the then ravenous dogs. He had been tied in such a way that the

full weight of his body was on his wounded feet. The
pain was so intense that at one point he fainted. How
long he had been unconscious he did not know but
when he came to, it was already dawn. All was still.
The guards dozed and even the hounds, exhausted with
howling, were fitfully asleep.

Down in the valley, in the hush of dawn, the Great
Bear could hear the first birds singing; thrushes, robins,

chaffinches, blackbirds, larks, sang with an intensity as though they were discovering their voices for the first time. They seemed to be singing away the blackness of the night and welcoming the sun which had not yet risen. The lake lay still, slate dark, reflecting the heavy mists that always hid the mountain's peak.

The pain stabbed through his feet like sudden knife wounds. And he was powerless to do anything. All the old spells were in the books inside his hut. And the few that he could remember could not help him. He knew that the treasure was somewhere inside the mountain but he doubted that he would now remember where exactly it was hidden; he rather hoped he would not. Even if he did, he knew there was no question of his revealing its whereabouts. He would die sooner than betray his trust. Yet at the same time he realised that Malevil's forces were so highly organised that it was only a matter of time before he succeeded in levelling the mountain. Below him he could see the great cranes and huge trucks clearing away the falls of rock caused by the explosions which, at intervals, shook the mountain.

He wished he could remember what the treasure was. Obviously it had been important enough to have been guarded all these centuries, awaiting the destined time when it should be revealed. Malevil had told him that the Lost Treasure of Wales was worth more than all the copper and gold mines of Africa. The Great Bear shuddered to think he could have been so careless. If only Merlin were here and could once again rescue him.

O Great Merlin! cried the Great Bear silently within himself. *Come to my aid!* There was no one else to whom he could turn. Had he been free he might have been able to get a message to Farmer Thomas and his brother and then they would have got a message to Ursus Minor, the Little Bear. What was his other name? Odd! Though what one small bear and two farmers could hope to achieve against the forces of Malevil was more than doubtful.

By now the sky had turned a faint blue with wisps of cloud, and the mists in the valley were slowly lifting.

The sun at that moment appeared, a disc of light so intense and dazzling that the Great Bear had to close his eyes.

When he opened them he saw, perched on the bars of the cage, a small white owl. At first he thought perhaps it was a trick of the light, and that he was merely seeing a reflection of the rising sun on the bars of the cage. But when he looked again, the owl was still perched, motionless, its eyes large and unblinking, its white and cream

feathers shining in the sunlight. For a few moments the Great Bear no longer saw the owl because his eyes were misted with tears. For this was Taliesin, Merlin's owl.

The owl gave a soft, trembling hoot, as its head turned sharply to look down at the sleeping dogs. Then, silently, it lifted its wings and was gone, down, down, into the shadowed valley like a mote of sunlight.

The Great Bear felt as though he, too, had taken wing and somehow his pain, though no less, seemed now more bearable. He was not alone after all. Somewhere, somehow, Merlin had heard his prayer and sent both a silent message and a messenger.

Far off, lights flashed, one after the other, moving rapidly. In the valley people were already travelling to work, the rising sun reflected on the windscreens of their cars. From the chimney of his small hut smoke was now rising where someone had lit a fire. Other guards stumbled forth yawning, and went to splash their faces in the lake, before going to take over from the previous guard. The hounds awoke, stretched, and their barking set echoes ringing.

'You ready to talk yet?' said one of the men, poking the Great Bear through the bars with a stick.

'Best leave him till the Boss comes. He doesn't like his prisoners being mucked about with. Anyway, it's time we opened the next set of gates!'

Farmer Thomas was sitting on the step outside the big
barn, watching the sun come up. His left eye, as always
happened when he was tired, was bloodshot. He patted
Rover who lay at his side. Soon he would go in and
make a fresh pot of tea and take a cup up to Mrs
Thomas. Inside the barn were the ewes that had lambed
that night. Later he would take them down the lane to
a field where they would join the others.

He looked at the sky, screwing up his eyes against
the sun where he had noticed a dark speck, the size of
a moth, travelling through the sky. At the same moment
Odd, who had woken early, came running across the
yard. Then he, too, saw the moving shape, nearer now
and almost on top of him. Because the sun dazzled his
eyes he could not see what it was. Against the sun, with
outspread wings, it now seemed huge and dark. Odd
wondered if it was an eagle. He had often heard Farmer
Thomas describe how in these parts an eagle would
swoop suddenly out of the sky and snatch up a young
lamb. Now, as its shadow fell across him, he cried out in
fright. Feeling the rush of air from its wings he hid his

face in his paws and curled up on the ground.

He lay there, quite still. Then, in the silence, he heard a soft trembling, *Whoooo!*

'It's all right, Odd!' called Farmer Thomas, his boots clattering over the flagstones. 'It's only a barn owl. Don't be frightened.'

Odd looked up. The owl was perched on the rail of a farm wagon looking solemnly at him. Its head swivelled. It looked at Farmer Thomas, then back at Odd. With its wings folded it was smaller than Odd. Now it lifted its wings again and circled the yard. Farmer Thomas and Odd stared up at it, wonderingly. The owl flew a short distance away. As it flew something tiny fell to the ground.

'It's one of the owl's pellets,' explained Farmer Thomas. 'You'll find the remains of its supper inside.'

Odd stood, holding the pellet in his paw. The owl flew on a bit further and dropped another pellet. Farmer Thomas picked it up. The owl flew further still

and dropped a third pellet.

'That's funny!' said Odd. 'It's almost as if it wants us to follow it.'

'I wonder?' murmured Farmer Thomas, rubbing his left eye which itched.

'What?' asked Odd, looking up at him.

'Did you notice which direction it came from?'

Odd stared at him. 'You mean?'

Farmer Thomas nodded. 'Yes. It came across Brockland Forest from the direction of Bear Mountain!'

'Do you think,' said Odd, 'that it might have something to do with the Great Bear? That it might be some kind of message?'

They both turned and looked at the owl which was now perched on the gate into the farmyard. Suddenly, swiftly, like the shutter on a camera, it winked; and then went on staring at them.

They moved closer and again the owl lifted up its wings and flew on ahead of them.

'There's no doubt about it!' said Farmer Thomas excitedly. 'It wants us to follow it.'

He looked down at Odd. 'I'll go and wake Dai and ask him if he'd mind doing the milking. Then we'll take the Land-Rover and see where it leads us.'

The owl led them to the far side of Brockland Forest. The forest covered many thousands of acres around the foot of Bear Mountain. Much of it had been cut down and replanted but the greater part remained, centuries old, with huge oak trees that were twenty or thirty feet around the trunk, and towering high into the sky.

They drove slowly along an old track, the owl alighting on a branch every hundred yards or so. Once

they saw in the distance, far inside the forest, an old ruin, like a fallen down church. As they drove slowly past it the owl hooted three times.

'What is that?' asked Odd, peering out with interest.

'It's an old chapel,' replied Farmer Thomas. 'My father used to say, and he heard it from his father, that that's where Merlin retired to live as a hermit.'

'What's that?' asked Odd. 'A hermit?'

'A hermit's a holy man who likes to live on his own,' explained Farmer Thomas. 'Merlin was a very wise man and people used to journey from all over the world to see him. Then suddenly he just disappeared. Perhaps he got fed up with having to see so many people all the

time. But he always said that one day he would return.'

Odd looked up at the owl. 'Perhaps Merlin will help us find the Great Bear,' he said, and at that moment the owl winked at him again.

'Perhaps he will, lad,' replied Farmer Thomas, as the owl flew on ahead, and they followed.

They had now reached a part of the forest where the trees grew so thickly together that only a dim green twilight filtered its way down from far above. In front of them, blocking the path, was a giant oak that had been felled. Beyond it were other trees that had also been felled, all blocking the track for as far as they could see.

'That's curious,' murmured Farmer Thomas. 'Do you see? They are newly felled.' He paused. 'It's almost as though someone didn't want this part of the forest used.'

Silently the owl alighted in front of them. Farmer Thomas looked at it thoughtfully and then said, 'We'll leave the Land-Rover here and travel the rest of the way on foot.'

From now on the owl flew high above them. They could no longer see it but were guided by its soft hoot. Slowly, sweating, their faces scratched and torn by branches and brambles and thorns, they stumbled their way forward until they came to a clearing where the track divided. The owl flew softly along the left-hand track and they followed.

'We must go very quietly,' said Farmer Thomas. 'I think we are coming to the edge of the forest. Watch where you put your feet. Don't tread on any twigs.'

Soon they came across the familiar notice boards announcing – *Danger! Keep Out! Private Property*. And then at last they saw the fence.

Beyond the forest the land rose steeply to the rocky

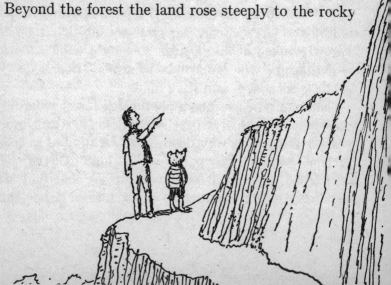

face of the mountain. Encircling the mountain was a
twelve foot high wire fence, with barbed-wire at the
top, curving outwards, and obviously electrified. At
intervals they could see guards marching up and down.
Suddenly there was an explosion. The ground trembled
and they heard, far up, an avalanche of rocks cascading.

'That's high explosive they're using,' whispered
Farmer Thomas. Above the noise of the blast, they
heard also the soft call of the owl and the next moment
it had flown over the fence and was soaring higher and
higher like a hawk.

'Oh, do you see?' whispered Odd. 'That's the way I
climbed up that first time. And there, at the top, only
we can't see it, is where the Great Bear's hut is. That's
where the owl is going. We've got to get there!'

Farmer Thomas shook his head. 'We wouldn't stand
a chance, Odd. Whatever's going on, we'd be shot at
sight, or arrested. We might have stood a chance by

night but . . . do you see? they've rigged up great arc-lamps all the way along, to floodlight the mountain.'

'But what about the Great Bear?' insisted Odd. 'Obviously he's in trouble else the owl wouldn't have brought us here.'

He looked up urgently and anxiously at his friend. Farmer Thomas rested a strong brown hand on his neck and smiled.

'We can't do it on our own, Odd,' he replied quietly. 'We need help. There's too many of them and too few of us. What we need is someone like Dr Morgan, and if you are agreeable I suggest we give him a ring and ask if we can go and have a talk with him after surgery this evening.'

'But why Dr Morgan?' asked Odd, as later that evening they climbed into the Land-Rover with Dai and drove down to the village

''Cos he always seems to know the answer to everything,' answered Farmer Thomas. 'Whether it's how to get wax out of your ears, or when's the right time of the year to plant petunias, or where flies go in the winter.'

'Where do flies go in the winter?' asked Odd, suddenly curious.

'Don't you know that?' laughed Dai. 'Why, they go to sleep under the floorboards!'

'Anyway,' added Farmer Thomas, 'Dr Morgan knows everybody and everything round here. If anything needs organising he does it. And it looks to me as though we're going to need every bit of help we can get.'

Inside the small waiting-room were red-faced farmers, an old lady with a plastic hearing aid, and two small children with spots and tired mothers. One boy had brought his dog. 'He's eleven and so am I!' he announced proudly.

At that moment the doctor popped his head round

the door. 'Who's next?' he called.

The boy rose.

'Hello, Christopher!' nodded the doctor. 'Who's sick this time, you or Bronco?'

When all the patients had gone, the doctor called them into his surgery and they sat round the gas-fire which popped and wheezed like an old man with pleurisy. He looked at Farmer Thomas and asked, 'How's the eye, Albert?'

'Not too bad, thank you, doctor. It's when I get over-tired that it becomes troublesome.'

The doctor nodded thoughtfully. Most of his patients were farmers and they all worked too hard.

He plugged in an electric kettle. 'We'll have a cup of coffee – with some rum to give it extra spirit!' He grinned. 'I told Mrs Morgan we might have some sandwiches later on. I thought we'd be more private in here than in the front parlour. Now tell me what it is you want to discuss.'

The doctor listened carefully while Farmer Thomas and Odd told him everything they knew. He seemed particularly interested in Odd's description of the way up to the Great Bear's hut. When they had finished he asked Farmer Thomas to do him a drawing of Bear Mountain.

'I'm not much of an artist!' he grinned, sucking the end of a thick pencil.

'I just want to get an idea of where the fences are placed as well as the general layout,' explained the doctor.

While Farmer Thomas concentrated on the drawing, his tongue sticking out between his teeth, Dr Morgan got out various Ordnance Survey maps and, having found the right one, began to mark in the whereabouts of the fences in red ink.

When Farmer Thomas had finished, the doctor compared the drawing and the map. He sighed and leaned back, tapping his teeth with the red Biro. Glancing across at the two men he asked, 'Do you know Fred Horgan?'

'Do you mean Fred, your gardener?' replied Dai.

'That's the man. I think we ought to bring him in on this.'

Albert and Dai looked at each other and then across at Odd. They felt it was very much up to him to decide.

'We need help,' replied Odd. 'Although it isn't

numbers that's going to help us against whatever forces are behind all this.'

The doctor looked shrewdly at him. 'Hmm!' he grunted. 'You seem to have your head screwed on the right way, lad!'

He was silent for a moment and then he continued. 'The point about Fred Horgan is that he used to work for the Water Board and he knows every underground tunnel in this part for fifty miles or more. Each year he used to have to walk the tunnels to check that there were no cracks or faults in the fabric. Of course they switched off the water at the reservoirs first!' he added with a chuckle.

'But if they switched off the water,' said Dai, 'surely that would mean no one would get any water while the tunnel was being walked?'

'Yes, that's what I don't understand either,' agreed Farmer Thomas.

'It doesn't work quite like that. Take the main water supply to Birmingham, for example', explained Dr Morgan. 'They only shut off a section of the tunnel at a time, perhaps a five mile stretch. There are entrances at regular intervals which can be entered from above ground by means of a man-hole. The linksman, as he is called, will enter one section where the water has been turned off, walk along that for five miles and then climb out at the man-hole. And so on. Do you get the idea?'

They nodded.

'But what has all this to do with our rescuing the Great Bear?' asked Odd.

'If I remember rightly,' answered the doctor, 'there used to be an underground tunnel somewhere between

Brockland Forest and Bear Mountain. It's disused now but I'm sure I've heard Fred say it went under the mountain. If that is so then there may well be a way on to the mountain from *inside*. Do you see what I'm getting at?'

'You mean,' said Odd excitedly, 'that we wouldn't have to go anywhere near the fences or the guards because we might be able to find a way from the tunnel up into the inside of the mountain!'

At that moment there was a tap on the door and Mrs Morgan looked round it to say, 'Fred Horgan is asking whether you want him to get any more shrubs for you from the nursery when he's passing it tomorrow?'

'Oh, tell him to come in here. He's just the man we need.'

In no time at all Fred Horgan had grasped the situation and sat down to study the doctor's map. He whistled while he rolled a cigarette. The tobacco hung in loose ends and flared up when he lit it. He blew out a cloud of smoke which was so strong that Odd choked. Dr Morgan had to open the window and Fred Horgan put out his cigarette.

'Sorry, lad!' he apologised, grinning. 'I ought to have known better. The missis always makes me smoke in the garden shed. That's how I came to take up gardening. The missis wouldn't allow me in the house.'

He looked up from the doctor's map.

'There is an old disused tunnel under the mountain although what condition it's in now, I can't say. It had to be closed down because of seepage from the lake at the top of the mountain.' He paused and looked round at the others. 'I take it you're willing to count me in on this?' he grinned.

'Oh, yes!' they chorused.

'Right then! Now there is a small natural tunnel, no more than a passage, which leads from the lake at the top of the mountain down into the main tunnel. That passage is too small for a man but ...' and here he looked across at Odd, '... a small bear could manage it!'

Odd's heart thumped. Once before he had climbed the mountain and nearly lost his life. That had been on the outside and now here he was being asked to climb the mountain from the inside, up a passage that no one had ever climbed before him.

'But supposing the passage is flooded out?' questioned Odd.

'That we shan't know until we get there,' answered Fred. 'Apart from that shower earlier today it's been pretty dry the last two weeks, so that we may be lucky.'

He paused, looking gravely round at the small gathering. 'This could be dangerous. I think you ought to know that. The roof could suddenly cave in or we could be drowned. And the worst of it is that once Odd starts the long climb up to the lake we shall have no way of maintaining contact with him. If he gets stuck we've no way of getting help to him.'

They looked at Odd solemnly.

And Odd looked back at them. 'Of course it's dangerous,' he said. 'But we don't really have any choice. Do we?

'That's the spirit, boy bach!' laughed Fred.

The door opened and Mrs Morgan came in with a tray of food. 'I've brought some sandwiches for you men, and Odd, I've brought you some milk and honey. I think you need building up!'

'Oh, I mustn't get too fat,' stammered Odd, 'else I might get stuck!'

Later that night the small band assembled up at the farm. Mrs Thomas and the children were to take care of any lambs that might be born. Those ewes that were expected to lamb soon had been gathered into a straw-covered yard next to the old barn. Arc-lamps, hung on lengths of cable, were strung across, floodlighting the swollen ewes with their dark glittering eyes and white bony faces. Some stood gravely munching; others moved slowly about, or knelt, patiently assembled and waiting like a congregation in a large cathedral. There was a sense of stillness, of expectation about the whole scene, broken only by the occasional bleating of lambs inside the barn.

Mrs Thomas and the children waved quietly as first the doctor and Fred Horgan set off, leading the way, followed by Albert and Dai Thomas and Odd in the Land-Rover. The children did not know where they were going; but they had been told it was to do something very important.

At the edge of the forest they parked their vehicles and followed Fred on foot.

'We'd best try not to use the flashlights,' said Fred. 'The entry to the tunnel is about half a mile from here.'

Ahead of them they could see Bear Mountain, its steep side illuminated by the sweeping searchlights which moved across it at regular intervals.

The entrance to the tunnel was down a man-hole. Around it had grown up a spinney of ash and hazel which now acted as a cover. Fred inserted a master key into the man-hole but it refused to open. Odd looked at him in consternation.

'Are you sure you brought the right key, Fred?' asked the doctor.

Sweat ran down Fred's forehead as he twisted and turned the long piece of metal like a poker.

'It's the right key,' he grunted, 'but it's a long time since this man-hole was opened and it's fair rusted up.'

Suddenly the lid yielded and Fred nearly fell backwards. He wiped his sleeve across his forehead, breathing heavily.

'I'll go first,' he said. 'And then Odd. And whoever's last must make sure the lid is lowered behind him. We don't want anyone to come across an open man-hole and get curious!'

They climbed down a narrow ladder inside a metal pipe that measured about two feet across and seemed to descend for a long way into the earth. Down, down they went. It was like going down a well. The echo of their feet on the iron rungs was deafening, while the smell of warm, stale air nearly choked them. Then Fred was shining his torch and Odd, standing next to him, saw that they were on a platform with steps leading down into a tunnel that stretched ahead of them for as far as they could see. Moisture oozed from the stone walls and the lower part of the tunnel was submerged in water.

'Seepage!' observed Fred. 'That's why this tunnel had to be closed. A lot of it here. However, I think this is mainly from yesterday's shower and, as I said, it shouldn't be too bad after the dry spell we've had lately.'

They moved forward in single file, lifting their feet high as they travelled along the slippery base of the tunnel, water sloshing and swirling. Farmer Thomas carried Odd on his back. None of them spoke, each concentrating on keeping his balance. After about half an hour Fred halted.

'This is it!' he whispered.

As he flashed his torch forward they could see that the tunnel was partly blocked by a fall of stone over which the water cascaded. Above, in the roof, to one side, was an opening through which the moisture trickled over a ledge of green slime.

Farmer Thomas lowered Odd who stood, above the level of the water, on the pile of fallen rocks.

Fred turned and looked at him. 'It's up to you now, young man,' he said quietly. 'You're the only one who can get up there. And even so, none of us knows what you'll find for no one has ever been up there.'

He stooped and picked up a handful of pebbles. 'Put these in your pocket. And every so often drop one down just to let us know everything is all right. All set?'

Odd looked round at the four anxious faces watching him and then removed his scarf. 'I think I'd best leave this behind,' he said.

With a grin, Fred lifted him up and inserted him into the opening like a fox terrier being put down a badger's earth. There was a shower of small stones, a trickle of water, and then Odd was gone. For a long time they could hear him scrabbling away like a rat. After that there was a silence.

'Cigarette?' suggested Dai.

He and Albert lit up. The doctor said he did not smoke. Fred rolled one of his own.

'Do you think it wise, Fred?' grinned Dai. 'You might smoke us out of here!'

They were just stubbing out their cigarettes when suddenly there was a loud crack, as though a gun had gone off. Each of them held his breath, listening intently. The next moment there was a fierce rattle followed by a shower of dust and a small stone fell out of the opening and went plop! into the water.

The four men looked up at the opening too small for man or boy and sighed with relief.

'At least he's on his way!' laughed Fred. 'I reckon that's worth another cigarette!'

68

There was no light in the tunnel but bears have a keen sense of smell and Odd chose to rely on this rather than use his torch. He had no idea how long he would be in the tunnel and he might have more urgent need of the torch later on.

He crawled slowly, on hands and knees, as the tunnel twisted and turned. It was like climbing up the slope of a helter-skelter, he thought, and would be a lot easier coming down!

He wondered how far inside the mountain he had to go. It must be at least seven miles long and he had no idea how high it was. As he inched forward in the darkness he found himself murmuring the words of an old song that Collander Moll used to sing. Perhaps she was singing it even now, as she went about her spring-cleaning. Of course she wouldn't, he corrected himself, because this is the middle of the night. She'll be in bed, he giggled to himself, with her wigs on the bed-posts on either side, and snoring!

How many miles to Babylon? he sang inside himself. He did not dare make a sound lest it should echo and be heard at the other end, and alert the guards.

Three score miles and ten, he answered himself.

Can I get there by candle-light? He paused to check that the torch was still in his pocket.

Yes, and back again.

If your heels are nimble and light,
You may get there by candle-light.

He wondered if he would be back by dawn. Suppose he got lost and could not find his way back at all? Suppose he were trapped inside the mountain? No one would be able to rescue him.

Suddenly he came to a halt. There was rock in front of him and on either side. The tunnel had come to an end in a cul-de-sac. For a moment he felt relieved. There would be no disgrace in going back now. He had merely come to the end of his journey sooner than he had expected. He took out his torch just to check. Yes, there was solid rock; but then the light flickered across a wetness. Following its direction he saw that the tunnel continued upwards. Above him loomed a shaft like a tall chimney. He risked shining the light up it

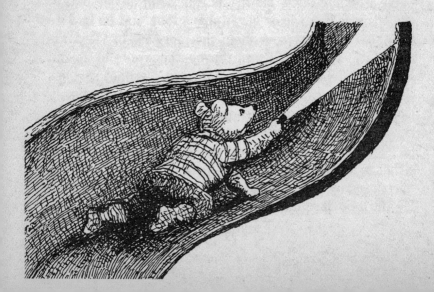

but it seemed to soar upwards and upwards. He switched off the torch. He knew he had no choice but to go on. He pulled himself up until he was wedged inside the shaft and then, slowly, foothold by handhold, pushed his way upwards. He could not even look down, which was perhaps as well since he did not have a good head for heights. Then a horrid thought struck him and he nearly let go as his stomach heaved with fright: there would be no coming down this shaft without a rope. And he had none. But the thought of his four friends waiting anxiously below, and of the Great Bear possibly waiting up above, gave him heart and he climbed steadily on until he had reached the top of the chimney.

He took one of the small stones from his pocket, and let it drop down the shaft. He listened as it went clattering down, bouncing from side to side. It made such a clatter that he decided he must not risk this again, lest he should give away his presence. Even now he wondered anxiously whether the sound would have travelled upwards, so that, whoever was up there would have warning of his approach and lie in wait to catch him as he came out of the tunnel.

He got up quickly. It was not good to have thoughts like these. It was better to keep moving.

Carefully he switched on the torch, shading it with one paw. He saw that he was sitting on a shelf of rock and that the tunnel continued on the opposite side of the shaft. He counted three and jumped across but just as he landed on the other side his feet slipped and he fell backwards. He grabbed at the rock-face for support and, as he did so, the torch slipped from his paw and went clattering down the chimney, its light flickering from side to side, until the glass smashed and then he saw it no more.

This accident upset his nerve very badly. Not only had he given away his presence by making so much noise, but he had lost the torch. From now on he would have to rely on smell and touch. And taste. He would have to imagine that he was a blind bear. It wasn't the end of everything, he told himself.

Quite soon he found the tunnel divided and he followed the damper of the two. It divided many times, until he found he had lost count of how often this had happened. He would never be able to find his way back. But he had given up worrying. All that mattered was that he should keep on until he came out of the mountain into the daylight and fresh air.

Once he stopped, his heart thumping. He could have sworn he heard whispering and the sound of feet. He stayed quite still, listening, then slowly he moved on. It must have been his imagination, the effect of tiredness and strain, and being in the dark for so long.

After several hours he felt something caress his face. At first he thought it must be bats. He did not realise that it was light, filtering through from ahead. And with the light there came a moistness and a freshness.

The tunnel was now large enough for him to be able to walk upright and he could see the sides of the rock. There was no colour to anything, just a floating greyness which he gradually realised was a swirling mist.

The next moment he was standing on the pebbled shore of a small lake. He stood quite still, trying to sense his whereabouts. Had he gone right through the mountain and come out on the other side, or had he really reached the top where the Great Bear lived in his stone hut beside the mountain loch? Slowly and cautiously he moved along the shore. Suddenly he saw something looming up at him out of the mist. It was like the spokes of a giant umbrella without any covering but with a hole in the middle. Inside, on a pole, where the handle of the umbrella would have been, hung a dark shape.

There seemed to be something familiar about that dark shape, but at first he could not imagine what it was or what a giant umbrella was doing up on Bear Mountain. There was no sound or sight of anyone. Everything was very hushed and silent in the fog. The mountainside seemed deserted. Except for that figure hanging from the pole.

Then he heard a sound. It was a sigh, but a deep sigh. He moved closer to the figure until he was right underneath it.

Suddenly, the tears shot to his eyes and he cried out, 'Oh, Great Bear, Great Bear! What is it? What have they done to you?'

There was no answer.

'It's me, Odd,' he persisted. 'You know, Ursus Minor. Please tell me what can I do for you? Tell me, tell me!'

The tears ran down his cheeks.

Haltingly, jerkily, as though in great pain, the figure whispered, word by word, 'They – will – kill – me.'

'Who will?' asked Odd.

'Malevil and his followers.'

'But why?'

'Unless I tell them where the treasure is hidden, they will kill me. I have forgotten where the treasure is hidden, but you remember. You know where it is. You tell them. If you tell them they will spare me and I . . .'

Here the figure broke off with a cry of pain. Odd stared up at the Great Bear, puzzled.

75

'Great Bear,' he said, very gently, 'Don't you remember, you forgot where it was hidden and that's why we never found it.'

'You lie!' screamed the figure suddenly. And at that moment something terrible happened. It was as though the Great Bear's face fell in and another face took its place; a face he did not know, the mouth screaming at him, and one eye bulging. At that very moment, when Odd found himself staring into the evil face of a man wrapped in an animal skin, he was seized from behind by guards.

Oh, stupid, stupid, stupid! he cried to himself. How could he not have foreseen this? He had walked straight into a trap. But where was the Great Bear? Was he a prisoner? Or had he been killed and was that his skin which this man was wearing? He stared at the man's face, hypnotised. It was calm now, cold and mask-like. Then a smile flickered across it, like a whip flashing through the air.

'Welcome, Ursus Minor! I am Malevil.'

The four men had waited anxiously through the long hours of that night, not knowing whether Odd was on his way back or had even reached the end of his journey. When finally the smashed torch had shot out into the main tunnel they had been very worried. What did it mean?

'We could be sitting here for days on end,' remarked Fred, 'and be none the wiser, and Odd in real trouble.'

'If only we knew what was happening at the other end!' added Farmer Thomas.

Dr Morgan looked up suddenly. 'You've given me an idea, Albert. If Dai and Fred don't mind keeping guard here while you and I drive back to my house, I've got some very powerful binoculars there. We might then be able to see something of what is happening up on the mountain.'

They were driving along the road in the moonlight when they noticed ahead of them a tall dark figure limping along.

'I don't like the look of that chap,' observed Farmer Thomas. 'Big ugly brute. You get all types on the road nowadays. I wouldn't stop for the likes of him.'

Suddenly Farmer Thomas began to slow down.

'What's the matter?' queried the doctor. 'You're not going to stop are you, Albert?'

'That's funny,' muttered Farmer Thomas to himself. 'I could swear . . .' He stopped the Land-Rover and jumped out.

'It is!' he cried out excitely. 'It's the Great Bear!'

The Great Bear looked dazed. He stumbled and nearly fell.

'He seems almost done in,' observed the doctor. 'Goodness, look at those feet!'

Farmer Thomas looked down at the Great Bear's feet. The bandages were unravelled, stained with blood and dirt.

The Great Bear smiled. '*To be among friends,*' he said, '*is a sign that spring is on its way*. A saying of Merlin's!' he added. Then he fell, like a tree.

Back on the farm, Mrs Thomas bathed the Great Bear's

feet; the doctor applied ointments and fresh bandages, and gave him some pills to swallow with a glass of water.

'To lessen the pain a little,' he explained.

'But how did you manage to escape?' asked Dr Morgan after the Great Bear had described how he had been imprisoned.

'Really that was not so difficult,' answered the Great Bear. 'I noticed that both the men and the dogs fell asleep just before dawn, and I knew that if I wanted to escape it would have to be then or not at all. By degrees I managed to loosen the ropes that bound my hands and feet. Then I climbed to the top of the pole. I knotted a loop in one end of my scarf and managed to throw it over one of the spikes at the top of the cage. Once I'd done that it was just a matter of tying the other end to the pole, swinging my way across, and climbing down the outside of the cage. Of course every moment I expected that one of the dogs would hear me, but the mists were very heavy this morning, and that helped to muffle sound as well as to conceal what I was doing.'

He paused, sipping at the hot lemon and rum that Mrs Thomas had made for him. 'After that it was fairly straightforward. There are lots of old tunnels in the mountain. By using them I was able to escape the fences and the guards. In fact I came out by Merlin's old chapel in the forest. If those fools only knew it, the mountain is honeycombed with tunnels. In Merlin's day we used them a lot.'

All this while there had been a murmuring, like the swarming of bees, outside the door.

'Oh, drat those children!' sighed Mrs Thomas. 'They keep pestering me to let them see "the big bear", as they call you, sir.' She found she could not help referring

to the Great Bear as 'sir'.

'That's all right,' smiled the Great Bear, lying back in the arm chair. 'Let them come in.'

So Mrs Thomas ushered the children into the room. 'Only for a minute, mind now,' she said, clucking and fussing.

The seven children stared shyly up at the Great Bear.

Now that they were in the room they were over-awed
and a bit giggly. They looked at the bandaged feet of the
Great Bear. His brown eyes twinkled at them over the
tops of the new pair of National Health spectacles
the doctor had found for him.

'Are you really a Bear?' asked Stephen, gazing up
into the hairy face that reminded him a little of his

grandad who was also very old.

'Yes, I really am a bear.'

'Are you the Great Bear?' asked Jane.

'Yes, I am the Great Bear,' he answered.

'And what is Odd?' asked Stephen.

'He is the Little Bear,' came the answer.

'Great Bear and Little Bear,' said Jane to herself.

There was a pause and they were happy to be silent, gazing up at him.

'Come on now!' said Mrs Thomas suddenly, gathering them into a huddle and pushing them towards the hall. 'You don't want to tire the poor gentleman!'

They could hear her voice as she closed the parlour door.

'Now you'll be able to tell your children, and your grandchildren, how you met the Great Bear!'

'And the Little Bear!' Jane reminded her.

'And the Little Bear,' nodded her mother.

The door closed.

'How is Odd?' asked the Great Bear.

Farmer Thomas then told him how, at that very moment, so far as they knew, Odd was inside the mountain on his way to find him. The Great Bear rose and moved slowly to the window, looking out at the range of mountains with Bear Mountain in the background. When he turned, his face was very grave.

'It is really Odd who is in danger,' he said, 'much more than I. That is what I came to warn you.'

'But what can they hope to gain from a small bear?' asked Farmer Thomas. 'After all, he doesn't know the whereabouts of the treasure, whereas there is always the possibility that you might suddenly remember where it is.'

The Great Bear shook his head. 'Malevil does not yet know about Ursus Minor,' he answered. 'But when he does he will realise that he is the one who was destined to wake me and to whom the secret of the treasure is to be revealed. By now he may even have discovered this, or Odd may have told him without realising who Malevil is.'

For a moment he paused. The others could see that he was very troubled.

'Although I have forgotten the whereabouts of the treasure,' he continued, 'it will be revealed to Odd in Merlin's own good time. Malevil will realise this and try to use Odd for his own ends. At all costs we must rescue Odd. We are dealing with the powers of darkness. They are many and we, alas, are few. Or seemingly so!'

He broke off abruptly, moving with surprising speed to the window. Then he crossed to the door and was out of the house before Farmer Thomas and Dr Morgan realised what was happening.

Outside, in the moonlight, perched on the barn-door, was the owl.

'I was forgetting Taliesin, Merlin's Messenger!'

murmured the Great Bear. 'I was in danger of forgetting Merlin. With his aid we shall overcome. But we have no time to lose.'

He raised an arm. 'Welcome, Taliesin!' he cried. At once the owl flew down on to the outstretched arm.

The Great Bear spoke to him in a language none of them understood. While he was speaking, Taliesin closed his eyelids as though intently listening. When he had finished, Taliesin opened them suddenly, gave a soft *chirr*, and rose up into the air. Then he had gone.

The Great Bear turned back towards the small band which now included Mrs Thomas and the children.

'I hope he understood me!' he muttered. 'My Old Speech is a bit rusty, it's so long since I had to use it. I've sent him to get help, although how long it will take I don't know. We must wait patiently.'

'And will you tell us a story while we wait, Great Bear?' croaked Stephen.

'Now you're not to trouble Sir!' chided Mrs Thomas.

The Great Bear smiled. 'But I should like to,' he replied. 'It's a long time since I had anyone to tell a story to!'

So Mrs Thomas herded them into the barn where there was a paraffin heater. Soon she was handing hot drinks all round and distributing rugs and blankets.

'It's like a picnic!' said Jane.

The children sat at the feet of the Great Bear while Stephen held Greedy Guts in his arms. He looked up at the Great Bear.

'Once upon a time . . .' he prompted, seeing that the Great Bear seemed uncertain how to start.

'Once upon a time,' began the Great Bear, 'there was a bear who lived in a forest . . .'

Once during that night Taliesin returned to inform the Great Bear that Odd had been taken prisoner but that not knowing what had happened to the Great Bear or where he was, Malevil seemed at a loss what to do. Taliesin had also been seen by Odd who now knew that help was on its way. Then Taliesin disappeared once again and the long wait continued.

In the meantime Farmer Thomas had driven off to collect Dai and Fred and now they were all assembled, anxiously watching the sky. Suddenly the Great Bear pointed to the east where the sky was already lightening. A small cloud was travelling towards them, then they observed other clouds flying from east and west, north and south, which began to merge into one great cloud that darkened the sky like nightfall. Like a continuous drum roll, they heard the steady beating of thousands of wings as the birds began to descend.

The owls were the first to come flying in: the Long-Eared Owl, the Short-Eared Owl, the Little Owl, and the Barn Owl. Behind them, swooping down like swallows, followed hundreds of small owls – these were

85

the Pygmy or Sparrow Owls. They were followed by the
large Tawny Owls with their sharp cry of *Kowitt!
Kowitt!* Last of all, and most magnificent, was the
Eagle Owl, two feet long, its wingspan more than five
feet. There were three hundred Eagle Owls, their yellow
and red feathers glowing like coals. They were visitors
to these parts, the strongest and most powerful of the
owls.

The owls were followed by the birds of prey. The
magnificent, mewing Honey Buzzard was there as well
as the Common Buzzard, the proud Goshawk and the
fierce Sparrowhawk; while, circling before landing,
came the Montagu Harriers, and a few, rare, Red Kites.
From the direction of the forest flew hundreds of
Peregrine Falcons, while high above them hovered the
Kestrels. Suddenly there was a flip and whirr of wings
as thousands of small birds came flying swiftly in,
zigzagging across the ground and soaring into the air,
noisy as starlings at dusk; these were the Merlins,
named after their Master.

Field after field, tree after tree, was covered with
birds, all massed in rows, filing into place, while in the
foreground, as though supervising their arrival, was
Taliesin. Mrs Thomas and the children and the four
men stood in the background. In front of them towered
the massive figure of the Great Bear, his rich brown fur
bronzed by the first rays of the sun. His deep voice
rang out as he spoke to the waiting birds in the language
which only they could understand. They answered him
with cries and calls, hootings and mewings which rose
and fell like the sound of a wind on moorland. Then, as
he raised his arm, they were silent. The Great Bear
spoke now in a language that all could understand.

'In the name of Merlin I summoned you,' he cried out. 'Through the magic of Merlin I invoked your aid. By the power of Merlin I now command you!'

The sun was now half way above the horizon, its dazzling light reflected in the thousands of bird eyes.

'Go with Taliesin!' he commanded. 'Go with Merlin's own messenger. Do that which must be done, in the name and the power and the magic of Merlin!' He stepped back and waited. Slowly, species by species, like blankets of feathers, they lifted into the air, rising higher and higher until the sky was again darkened. Then, like a plague of locusts, they flew in the direction of Bear Mountain.

Strapped high on the pole inside the cage, Odd could see them coming. Then, with a roar of wings, they were swooping down on the mountain side. Malevil and his men drew their guns and fired, again and again. But as birds fell, as many more took their places. The air was thick with wings. Taliesin flew in and pecked Odd's bonds until he was released.

Wooohooo! came the call of Taliesin, swooping, rising, darting, summoning the birds to different parts of the fray. Many of the guards dived into the loch and were drowned. Others fell to their deaths from mountain ledges.

What happened to Malevil no one knew. The last time Odd saw him he was being pursued by hawks and eagles, following him like a swarm of bees. Whether he escaped, or fell to his death, none could afterwards remember.

By the time Farmer Thomas and his small band arrived with the Great Bear the enemy had been routed.

'Well done, Ursus Minor!' cried the Great Bear. 'Though you have the body of a little bear you have shown the courage of a great bear. I am proud of you.'

He turned to speak to the assembly of birds, thanking them for what they had done that night. Raising both arms, he called on Merlin, in words that were centuries old:

> *'May Merlin ever be before us and behind us,*
> *Beneath us and above;*
> *May Merlin surround us on every side.*
> *May he be with us in our beginning*
> *And at our end!'*

With a wild crying, a mewing and a hooting, the birds rose up like thistledown on the wind and floated away. Taliesin remained until the last and then he, too, rose, circled above the group, and finally flew towards the rising sun.

'Do you think we shall see Malevil again?' asked Odd.

'Yes, little one,' replied the Great Bear. 'The powers of darkness are always with us. We shall hear from him again. And when that time comes the battle will be more bloody and more fierce.'

'Will you be staying up here?' asked Odd, looking round at the tiny mossed and thatched hut that had served the Great Bear as a home for many centuries. 'Now that you have really woken up!' he added.

The Great Bear smiled. 'I see that you are becoming percipient,' he remarked.

'What does that mean?' asked Odd. 'Percy – whatever it was you said.'

'Percipient? It means having perception, insight, noticing or sensing things. You are growing up very quickly.'

He lifted his head, sniffing the air. 'You are right. I shall not be staying here. Now that spring has arrived, and now that I am really awake, I am determined to enjoy it all. I'm going to move my books and cooking pots down to Merlin's ruined chapel in the forest. And Farmer Thomas has promised to let me have a couple of beehives, and I shall grow my own vegetables, keep a few hens for eggs, and make my own cider. I intend making the most of this spell. Oh, dear, did I say spell!'

Later that day Farmer Thomas and his brother

helped the Great Bear move his possessions, while Mrs Thomas drove Odd and the children into the nearby market town so that Odd could buy presents to take back to London for Hallelujah and Collander Moll and Elsewhere.

Once upon a time when buying presents, Odd had always bought things that he liked, which he wished people would give him for a present. Gradually, however, he had found that not everyone likes receiving pots of honey. Now he tried always to think what each person would like and that was much harder. After all, what did one give someone like Collander Moll?

'What about a saucepan or a frying-pan or a kettle?' suggested Jane.

'She's got all those,' replied Odd. 'Besides, I don't think I would have enough money.'

'Or a dish-cloth or a mop?' said Stephen.

'She's got them.'

'Or a pin-cushion?'

'She's got one.'

They wandered all round Woolworth's trying to find something. Stephen got very bored.

'She must be a millionaire,' he said, 'with millions and millions and millions of money if she's got everything!'

'How does she keep all her wigs on?' asked Allen suddenly.

Odd stopped and stared. 'Now that's an idea!' he exclaimed.

'What?' they chorused.

'Hair-nets!' he cried, and with that they all cheered so that the other shoppers in Woolworth's turned round in surprise to stare at them.

'Six hair-nets, please!' piped Odd, handing the money to the startled assistant who had never served a bear before.

'That's one present done!' he announced with glee.

For Hallelujah he bought a large box of very long matches.

'It always takes Hallelujah so long to light his pipe,' explained Odd, 'because ordinary matches keep going out, and even then he's always getting his fingers burned!'

'That's a splendid present!' laughed Jane, rattling the big box of matches.

For Elsewhere some special notepaper with envelopes to match was purchased so that he could write letters to all his friends.

'Them's what I call Useful Presents!' laughed Mrs Thomas who appeared at that moment, having been to do some other shopping. 'I'd much rather have a Useful Present any day than the kind that costs a lot of money and gets put away in a drawer or shoved to the back of a cupboard and never used. Useless Presents I call those!'

Suddenly there was a lot of giggling and whispers of 'did you get it?' and then Stephen croaked, 'We've got a present for you!'

He handed Odd a parcel.

'Open it!' cried Jane, jogging up and down with excitement.

By now everybody in Woolworth's had stopped to watch.

'Are they advertising for stockings or something?' asked one woman. 'Only I saw the little bear and I wondered.'

Odd held the bag in his two paws. It was very heavy. His brown eyes twinkled. 'Is it a bomb?' he asked. 'Will it jump? Or bite? Or go bang?'

'Oh, Odd, do hurry up and open it!' pleaded Jane in suspense.

'Odd opened the parcel, and there were four jars of Welsh honey!

'Just what I should have chosen for myself!' he grinned. 'How did you guess?'

When they came out of Woolworth's they discovered the High Street was crowded. People were lining the pavements on either side as down the centre paraded a circus. In the front marched a splendid band. They were followed by clowns somersaulting. There were cages of lions and tigers; Cossack princes riding on horseback; a lady covered in diamonds and riding side-saddle on a White Arab horse. There was also a fat woman wearing a snake round her neck like a fur; and chimpanzees on bicycles, blowing trumpets; and then came the elephants. Suddenly Odd noticed a clown on the back of one of the elephants waving at him, trying to attract his attention. He looked again and yes, it was Elsewhere!

Just then the elephant stretched down its trunk and circling it around Odd's waist, lifted him up above the people who were now laughing and applauding. For a moment he was on a level with the tops of houses. Startled sparrows and starlings flew up. Then the elephant's trunk curved back, the pressure of its hold relaxed, and he found himself standing, a little unsteadily, on the wrinkled hide of the elephant's back. Elsewhere flung his arms about him and they danced round, laughing and waving.

Odd whispered in Elsewhere's ear, who then whispered in the ear of the elephant. Once again it reached down its long trunk, curling it around Stephen who rose in the air, chortling with laughter. One after the other the elephant lifted the children up on to its back. The last Mrs Thomas saw of her family that day they were dancing on the back of an elephant, on their way to the big top.

And that was how the children came to meet Elsewhere and how they all celebrated the safe return of Odd and the Great Bear.

THE END